The Dunderheads Behind Bars

The Dun

derheads

BEHIND BARS

PAUL FLEISCHMAN

illustrated by **DAVID ROBERTS**

WALKER BOOKS
AND SUBSIDIARIES

LONDON · BOSTON · SYDNEY · AUCKLAND

First published 2012 by Walker Books Ltd
87 Vauxhall Walk, London SE11 5HJ

2 4 6 8 10 9 7 5 3 1

Text © 2012 Paul Fleischman
Illustrations © 2012 David Roberts

The right of Paul Fleischman and David Roberts to be identified as author
and illustrator respectively of this work has been asserted by them
in accordance with the Copyright, Designs and Patents Act 1988

This book has been typeset in Esprit

Printed in China

British Library Cataloguing in Publication Data:
a catalogue record for this book is available from the British Library

ISBN 978-1-4063-3655-9

www.walker.co.uk

For Julian and Sadie
P. F.

For my friends
D. R.

When school ended, I thought we were finished with our teacher, Miss Breakbone, for ever. I thought summer would be boring. I thought I'd never see the inside of a gaol cell.

Wrong, wrong again and very wrong. Maybe the other Dunderheads shouldn't call me Einstein.

It all began exactly on 12 July, on page 8.

I went over to Hollywood's to tell her the news. She's a five-star film nut. Summer gave her time to catch up on her filing.

"Ashley Throbb-Hart? Here? Omigod! I just left my nine hundredth comment on her blog! We're like, practically, you know—"

"People who've never met?"

She tried to mute me. It didn't work.

We ran into town with Spider to sign up as extras. Half the city seemed to be there.

"How far to the front of the queue?" asked Hollywood.

Spider's a champion climber. He shot up the nearest tall object. "Another half-mile."

Then the tall object turned.

"Mannerless monkey!" shrieked Miss Breakbone. **"Get off me this instant! I could have you arrested!"**

Her brother was the police inspector.
We moved back a few places in the queue.

We finally made it to
the front and got hired
for the park scene.

The hurricane scene was a problem
for Miss Breakbone.

We found Ashley Throbb-Hart's trailer
but could never get near her.

A few days later, I noticed some more news in the paper.

CAT BURGLAR STRIKES AGAIN

Priceless Necklace Taken From Third-Floor Bedroom

Citizens Demand Police Find Culprit

4th Jewel Theft This Week

I went to Spider's to see if he'd heard about it.
I wasn't the only visitor.

"Thanks for the tip," I heard Inspector Breakbone say. Our old teacher grinned.

"Where's the evidence?" I demanded.

"The kid's a climber," said Inspector Breakbone. "I don't need more proof. Or some kid telling me how to do my job."

"Especially this meddling mush-brain," said Miss Breakbone.

I called a meeting of the Dunderheads.

"Spider's mad about ropes,
not jewellery."

"Breakbone just wants to get back at us."

"I thought she toured with the Women's Wrestling League in the summer."

"We have to find the real thief," I said.

We visited Spider the next day. He had a ten-kilo weight on one leg to stop him from climbing out of gaol.

"Don't worry," I said. "We'll get you out. How's the food?"

"Awful," he said. "And I've heard my cell mate's in for cannibalism. So could you hurry?"

I thought ...

I measured ...

but I couldn't find a plan that worked. Then I remembered Google-Eyes was on holiday. I hoped her parents wouldn't mind if we used their empty house.

In the morning, I dropped in at Clips's place. "Got an express order for you."

"One hundred and eighty metres of three-strand? By Thursday?"

"It's that or Spider'll be somebody's dinner on Friday."

"I'll try," he said.

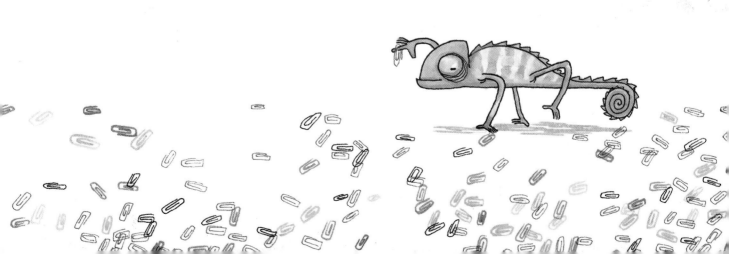

That afternoon, Pencil got to work on the flyer.

Wheels added auto-pedal to his bike that week. He made sure the word got out.

Junkyard combed his favourite alley.

32

Spitball had been teaching his dog tricks that summer.

I switched him to salami instead of wads of paper.

On Thursday morning I texted everybody: 2day@5.

Google-Eyes lives seven houses along from me.

Nails unlocked the back door with his right index finger.

We found her parents' bedroom upstairs.

Spitball got to work.

Junkyard had brought the jewellery box he'd found.

Clips attached the paper clips to it,

then we unrolled the chain all the way to my bedroom.

Everyone slept over.

The bell woke us up at 2.20.

I grabbed my phone and called the police.

"The cat burglar's just struck!" I gave them the address.

We ran down the block.
Junkyard studied the ground
round the pine tree.

"We're too late."

"No problem," I said. "Switch to Plan B."
Then Inspector Breakbone arrived.

"We got a call about a burglary in progress," he said. "I had a feeling you half-pint hooligans were involved." He didn't care that we were the ones who'd called. It took two cars to take us all to gaol.

They confiscated Pencil's pencils,

clipped Nails's nails,

and put us all in together.

Luckily, Spider's cell mate had gone.

In the morning, we were taken before a judge.

"Surely you youngsters can't be mixed up in this," he said.

"Actually," I replied, "we are. But in a good way."

I explained about the flyers, the paper clips and the jewellery box we'd set out as bait.

"Fine work," said the judge. "Too bad he escaped."

"We knew that might happen," I said. "So I got Spitball to rub salami on the room's floor. It'll be on the soles of the thief's shoes. All we need to do is let Spitball's dog track him."

The dog led the police from Google-Eyes's house all the way across town.

Finally, he stopped at one of the film crew's trailers. Which is how we caught the real thief –

the climbing …

crawling …

leaping stuntman

who'd been trying to win the love of Ashley Throbb-Hart with stolen jewellery.

"What was the best part?" a reporter
asked us two days later.

"The judge telling Inspector Breakbone
that he *could* use a kid's help."

"The mayor's Proclamation of Thanks."

"The private meeting with Ashley Throbb-Hart."

I thought it over. "For me, it was watching Spider walk out of gaol."